DOG TEAM SCOUTS

A WHITE HOUSE PROTECTION FORCE STORY

M. L. BUCHMAN

PRAISE FOR M. L. BUCHMAN

A fabulous soaring thriller.

— *TAKE OVER AT MIDNIGHT,* MIDWEST
BOOK REVIEW

Meticulously researched, hard-hitting, and suspenseful.

— *PURE HEAT,* PUBLISHERS WEEKLY,
STARRED REVIEW

Expert technical details abound, as do realistic military missions with superb imagery that will have readers feeling as if they are right there in the midst and on the edges of their seats.

— *LIGHT UP THE NIGHT,* RT REVIEWS, 4
1/2 STARS

Buchman has catapulted his way to the top tier of my favorite authors.

— FRESH FICTION

Nonstop action that will keep readers on the edge of their seats.

M L. Buchman's ability to keep the reader right in the middle of the action is amazing.

The only thing you'll ask yourself is, "When does the next one come out?"

The first...of (a) stellar, long-running (military) romantic suspense series.

I knew the books would be good, but I didn't realize how good.

Buchman mixes adrenalin-spiking battles and brusque military jargon with a sensitive approach.

— PUBLISHERS WEEKLY

13 times "Top Pick of the Month"

— NIGHT OWL REVIEWS

Tom Clancy fans open to a strong female lead will clamor for more.

— *DRONE*, PUBLISHERS WEEKLY

Superb! Miranda is utterly compelling!

— *BOOKLIST,* STARRED REVIEW

Miranda Chase continues to astound and charm.

— BARB M.

Escape Rating: A. Five Stars! OMG just start with *Drone* and be prepared for a fantastic binge-read!

— READING REALITY

The best military thriller I've read in a very long time. Love the female characters.

Other works by M. L. Buchman: *(* - also in audio)*

Action-Adventure Thrillers

Dead Chef
One Chef!
Two Chef!

Miranda Chase
Drone*
Thunderbolt*
Condor*
Ghostrider*
Raider*
Chinook*
Havoc*
White Top*
Start the Chase*

Science Fiction / Fantasy

Deities Anonymous
Cookbook from Hell: Reheated
Saviors 101

Single Titles
Monk's Maze
the Me and Elsie Chronicles

Contemporary Romance

Eagle Cove
Return to Eagle Cove
Recipe for Eagle Cove
Longing for Eagle Cove
Keepsake for Eagle Cove

Love Abroad
Heart of the Cotswolds: England
Path of Love: Cinque Terre, Italy

Where Dreams
Where Dreams are Born
Where Dreams Reside
Where Dreams Are of Christmas*
Where Dreams Unfold
Where Dreams Are Written
Where Dreams Continue

Non-Fiction

Strategies for Success
Managing Your Inner Artist/Writer
Estate Planning for Authors*
Character Voice
Narrate and Record Your Own Audiobook*

Short Story Series by M. L. Buchman:

Action-Adventure Thrillers

Dead Chef

Miranda Chase Origin Stories

Romantic Suspense

Antarctic Ice Fliers

US Coast Guard

Contemporary Romance

Eagle Cove

Other

Deities Anonymous (fantasy)

Single Titles

The Emily Beale Universe
(military romantic suspense)

The Night Stalkers
MAIN FLIGHT
The Night Is Mine
I Own the Dawn
Wait Until Dark
Take Over at Midnight
Light Up the Night
Bring On the Dusk
By Break of Day
Target of the Heart
Target Lock on Love
Target of Mine
Target of One's Own
NIGHT STALKERS HOLIDAYS
Daniel's Christmas*
Frank's Independence Day*
Peter's Christmas*
Christmas at Steel Beach
Zachary's Christmas*
Roy's Independence Day*
Damien's Christmas*
Christmas at Peleliu Cove

Henderson's Ranch
Nathan's Big Sky*
Big Sky, Loyal Heart*
Big Sky Dog Whisperer*
Tales of Henderson's Ranch*

Shadow Force: Psi
At the Slightest Sound*
At the Quietest Word*
At the Merest Glance*
At the Clearest Sensation*

White House Protection Force
Off the Leash*
On Your Mark*
In the Weeds*

Firehawks
Pure Heat
Full Blaze
Hot Point*
Flash of Fire*
Wild Fire
SMOKEJUMPERS
Wildfire at Dawn*
Wildfire at Larch Creek*
Wildfire on the Skagit*

Delta Force
Target Engaged*
Heart Strike*
Wild Justice*
Midnight Trust*

Emily Beale Universe Short Story Series
The Night Stalkers
The Night Stalkers Stories
The Night Stalkers CSAR
The Night Stalkers Wedding Stories
The Future Night Stalkers

Delta Force
Th Delta Force Shooters
The Delta Force Warriors

Firehawks
The Firehawks Lookouts
The Firehawks Hotshots
The Firebirds

White House Protection Force
Stories

Future Night Stalkers
Stories (Science Fiction)

The Emily Beale Universe
Reading Order Road Map

any series and any novel may be read stand-alone
(all have a complete heartwarming Happy Ever After)

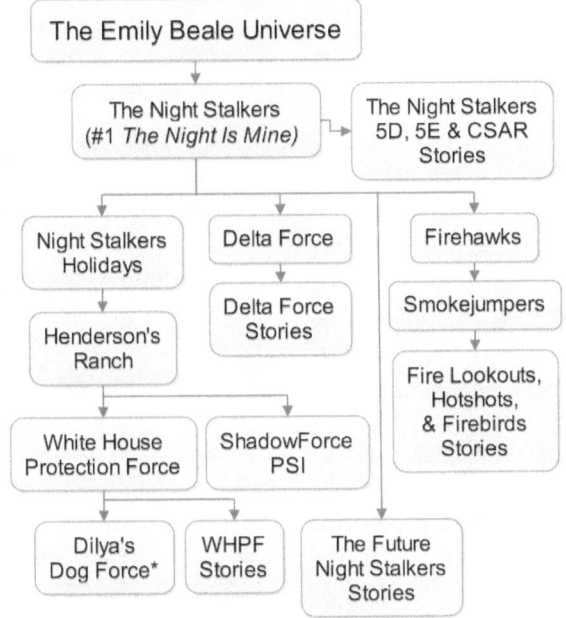

The Emily Beale Universe

The Night Stalkers
(#1 *The Night Is Mine*)

The Night Stalkers
5D, 5E & CSAR
Stories

Night Stalkers
Holidays

Delta Force

Firehawks

Henderson's
Ranch

Delta Force
Stories

Smokejumpers

White House
Protection Force

ShadowForce
PSI

Fire Lookouts,
Hotshots,
& Firebirds
Stories

Dilya's
Dog Force*

WHPF
Stories

The Future
Night Stalkers
Stories

* *Coming soon*
For more information and alternate reading orders, please
visit: www.mlbuchman.com/reading-order

ABOUT THIS BOOK

SOMETIMES BEING ALONE AND IN THE LEAD ROCKS.

Sometimes it doesn't.

US Secret Service Agent Nancy Sturgis and her sniffer-companion labradoodle, Iron, are used to going it alone. Their job? Pre-travel site security for the President.

Only Agent Harley Davis, logistics planning, moves out ahead of them.

After two years of knowing each other only through field reports, they are thrown together planning a major State visit to Senegal. Except before they truly begin, they're called to rush off and scout a crisis trip that must happen not within months, but in hours.

A heart-warming romantic suspense.

1

———————

NANCY STURGIS EASED HER WAY ONTO THE CROWDED HC-130J Super Hercules search-and-rescue plane. The massive cargo bay was packed to the limit by six 436L master pallets of emergency medical supplies. The fact that she knew the pallet spec made her brain hurt. If the Air Force issued frequent flyer miles, she'd long since have been set for life.

Other than the crew of four, she and her Secret Service sniffer-dog, Iron, were the only passengers. The Hercules wasn't off to search or rescue anyone tonight. Their flight would be crossing the Atlantic—conveniently at the same time she needed to do the same.

Over the last two years, she and her black labradoodle had traveled with: relief supplies, helicopters, tanks, entire companies of soldiers, spare airplane parts... About the only cargo that the Air Force flew that they hadn't traveled with was the Presidential Motorcade. She and Iron were the tip of the Presidential-travel advance scout spear. They were always onto the next site prep long before anything as mundane as the President and his Motorcade was involved. Not once since training had she even *seen* his Motorcade in action.

Well, they were *almost* the tip of the spear. Motorcycle Man, as she thought of Agent Harley Davis (assuming that was even his real name), was one step farther out. She'd read hundreds of his reports but never quite caught up with the man himself.

With a full load of pallets aboard, plus the search-and-rescue enhancements to the standard C-130, space was at a premium. She sat sideways on one of the few fold-down seats against the hull.

In the narrow space between her knees and the closest pallet, Iron shuffled back and forth. She was fine in flight, just two gals going about their business, but Iron never enjoyed the taxiing and take-offs.

If Nancy had been allowed to remove her muzzle and let her play with a toy, she'd probably have been fine. But dogs on military airplanes were muzzled when aboard. At least this crew didn't require the *box*. Iron hated being inside a dog carrier. She'd been well-enough trained to not complain but, when incarcerated, she had raised sad-puppy-dog eyes to an art form. On this load, the only real space to put a dog cage was atop the pallets and Iron would hate that even more.

"You're four years old now, Iron. Deal with it."

She rested her chin on Nancy's knee for about five seconds, but even an ear scritch didn't keep her in place. She paced to the end of her leash, turned, crossed by—once more treading on Nancy's toes—reached the closed rear ramp door, and turned again. Pacing.

Nancy tucked her feet back until her heels were touching the curve of the hull beneath her seat, leaned her head back, and closed her eyes. Every few seconds Iron brushed by her knees as the plane taxied.

Two years. They'd been in the field two years together. And, unusually for the Secret Service, almost always alone. They were so far out on point for the President's advance team that she often wondered why they hadn't run into the follow-up crew from some prior administration. If Iron had any space-time-continuum thoughts about that, she was keeping them to herself.

How lonely was Motorcycle Man? Harley didn't even have a dog to keep him company.

This trip had started like every other. The President's handlers had issued a *Possible Presidential Travel* notice. This time it was for a State visit tour six months out. That meant it was a major one. The smaller ones were okay but often frustrating as they were frequently canceled *after* all of the prep work was done. It was when there was an emergency somewhere, like a natural disaster, that life turned interesting. On those, the timeline from the advance scouts to full-on security lockdown abruptly compressed from weeks or months to hours.

But a major tour wasn't likely to be cancelled, which would be a relief. Though the aborted or changed-at-the-last-minute travel packages must be terribly frustrating for the teams downstream of her, they rarely affected her life. She and Iron would be long gone onto the next project by the time that could happen. It's what they'd signed up for. Well, she had. Iron hadn't had much choice.

By the motion of the plane's final turn, she knew they were at the head of the runway, though there were no windows back here. At the front of the cargo bay, big ones had been added to this model of the Hercules to allow for crew members to scan the ocean during SAR operations over the vast expanses they covered. Back here there was nothing but steel gray hull covered in fixtures for everything from emergency water and food for the crew in case of a remote crash, to life raft kits to dump out the rear ramp if survivors were spotted, to small cranes and who knew what all.

All four engines roared to full throttle. Takeoff time. Despite her heavy earmuffs, it was still harsh. Air Force planes never wasted payload on sound insulation except for VIPs. The bumping roll of acceleration replaced the easy sway of taxiing along. Iron buried her head between Nancy's knees. She covered Iron's floppy ears with her palms each time. But it was never the volume that appeared to make any difference to Iron, she hated even the quietest planes until they were airborne.

After a short roll, the Hercules floated aloft—it specialized in short landing-and-takeoff scenarios. With a loud hum and then a clank, the landing gear folded up and was locked away. Like a thrown switch, Iron raised her head, smiled at Nancy, then plopped down across her feet, pinning them awkwardly back against the hull.

This was going to be a long-haul flight. Hurlburt Field in Florida straight across to Africa.

Harley Davis would already have been there, sent out first to see if each stop *mandated* by DC was even logistically possible. If his report said yes, then she and

Iron were sent along in his wake to assess the scale of the required Secret Service prep team. Key question for her and Iron: could the sites be sufficiently secured to ensure the safety of the President of the United States? If not, could they make a shift sideways but still achieve the initial objective. If not, it was a scratch—no matter what whim had been issued by the politicos.

It was her and Harley's job to avoid another Ouagadougou Debacle. Her mentor had been on the team that had created the plan for President Clinton to visit the capital of Burkina Faso during a well-publicized tour of Africa.

It had been incredibly embarrassing to the Secret Service and to the President of Burkina Faso to cancel the visit with only a few weeks' notice. It turned out that the capital city of Ouagadougou simply didn't have enough hotel rooms for the five hundred people that made up a US President's security team and entourage. A poor, landlocked country in the part of Western Africa that was mostly the Sahara simply didn't have that kind of infrastructure back then.

The first stop of this trip was a shoo-in. Dakar, Senegal, at the westernmost tip of the African continent was a city of a million people. Four million in the greater metro area. At the heart of a peaceful country, it was a major financial center for Western Africa. There was also a Pan-African conference that the President was to address at a major conference center. It would require an inspection, but not much of one. The Dakar International Conference Center was a modern building with Presidential-level security and meeting spaces built into the design.

No, the catch was that the President was planning on being in the city for three days for meetings with individual leaders. When Presidents were in one place that long, it meant they wanted to see things—of course creating photo ops along the way. That vastly increased his exposure and it worried her. She had a long list of *possibles* to investigate.

Nancy managed to wedge her legs free from under Iron and rested them on her belly. She offered a happy sigh and they both settled in for the long flight—a Hercules traveled half the speed of an airliner.

2

IRON WANTED TO HIT THE GROUND RUNNING BECAUSE SHE'D slept through the whole flight per usual. Nancy hadn't managed a wink and could barely walk after the ten-hour overnight flight.

She stumbled down the ramp of the C-130 into the devastating heat. The President's trip was planned for the mild early spring months, which meant she was here in the blistering early fall. The dust off the Sahel that separated the Sahara from the rest of Africa made her eyes gritty by the third eyeblink. And the smothering humidity made sure that sweat sprang from her every pore to be instantly coated in more dust.

The first thing Nancy did was unclip Iron's muzzle so that she could pant to remove heat that way. Then she gave him a good rub along all of the muzzle's strap lines.

"How many minutes until we both look like we've been sweating red-orange mud?"

Iron looked up at her. Of course, she didn't sweat, so

she'd be able to clean her skin with a good shake. Then started panting...already.

Paying special attention to Iron's hydration and body temperature jumped to the top of her list. Thank goodness she'd been recently clipped. Dogs couldn't sweat through their skin, but their capillaries near the surface dilated when they grew hot. It moved their core heat to the surface to radiate away. A good spritz of cool water down Iron's back every now and then would help. Of course, then she'd have a *mud dog.*

"Fair play. If I have to, you have to."

She'd also better watch her own hydration. At the moment though, she was staggering from lack of sleep, not lack of water. She eyed her watch, eight o'clock a.m. local time. The sun was in the east and already baking the airport pavement. Experience had taught her that sleeping before it was nightfall wouldn't do her jetlag any favors—neither had the red-eye flight. She'd be in Africa for at least a week before continuing east as it was proposed as a Great Circle tour. So she'd best shift to this time zone. That meant staying awake until bedtime. It was going to be a damn long day.

Slinging on her pack, and carrying Iron's so that it didn't trap heat against her dog's back, she hustled toward the shade of a hangar. When she was a halfway across, she passed a small forklift that had seen better days, possibly, when it was being used to build the Parthenon.

As it pulled even with her, it stopped—in the sun.

To be polite, she stopped as well.

The driver was a tall Senegalese man with skin so

dark that his big smile was a slice of blinding white. He wore a white button-down shirt, dark slacks, and polished shoes. He looked more like an office worker than a forklift driver. Hanging onto the side was another man, wearing a far-more-sensible t-shirt, gym shorts, and flip-flops.

"You want to marry handsome Senegalese man." The driver said it like God's own truth.

Before she could protest, his companion spoke up.

"Then you want to be marrying me. Javier, he not so handsome as me. We will go to America, be very rich, and you will make me many babies."

Iron was more the cute and fluffy type of dog, with an exceptionally acute nose for explosives. He would attack on command, but he wasn't very scary to look at. Not scary at all really. At the moment, she wished for a snarling German Shepherd, twice Iron's size, and ready to back these annoying guys into the corner.

"I'm not marrying anyone." She turned and kept walking toward the hangar.

The driver backed up the forklift with an ease that proved he was indeed used to his machine no matter how he was dressed. He kept pace with her, ignoring the calls of the plane's loadmaster.

"We can get married next week. The imam is my cousin. It is no problem."

"What part of *no* didn't you understand?"

"Where in America do you live?" the second one asked. "I have many cousins in Atlanta. Yes. We will live in a big house in Atlanta near my cousins."

When a fuel truck driver rolled up on her other side

and proposed marriage, she began to wish for a pair of Rottweilers.

A man with blond hair and skin even lighter than hers slouched against the frame of the big hangar door, watching the whole scene. He was six-foot-one, probably making him shorter than any of these Senegalese, wore wrap-around shades, and the ubiquitous button-down, slacks, and, slight variation, rubber-soled leather shoes.

"I'm not marrying *you* either."

"Okay. Any particular reason?" His voice was as lazy as his slouch. But he offered a knowing smile that would only earn him an attack by an angry Corgi.

She waved a hand toward the overeager Senegalese.

He glanced up, then spoke softly, "She's with me."

"I am *not*." Though she waited until the other men had offered disappointed looks and headed off to do their tasks before she spoke.

"In this country, it's better if you are. Single white women are, by definition, rich. Wouldn't matter if you wore a wedding ring. If you had, the pitch would shift to *I am such a better man than your husband. Divorce him, marry me—*"

"*—and we'll move to Atlanta and you'll make me many babies.*"

His shrug didn't argue.

"And if I'm with you?"

"One, I won't be proposing marriage. Two, they'll leave you alone. A nice thing about Senegal is that while they're pushy, they'd never touch you. If a man touched a woman without invitation, he'd get the shit beaten out of him by the crowd."

"So they respect my body, just not me."

That earned her a half smile. "They respect and covet what you represent, the golden ticket out of Senegal and into the *perfection* of America. If it makes you any happier, there is *some* degree of altruism involved. They want the riches of America so that they can send money home to their families."

Nancy closed her eyes and counted to ten. It didn't help. Whatever she wanted, it wasn't any of that. Nor was it this smug stranger who so loved explaining things to her.

When she opened her eyes, he'd squatted down and was introducing himself to Iron who was eating it up.

"I don't need *you* either." She and her dogs had scouted routes in thirty-six of the fifty states and over forty countries all on her own, thank you very much.

Then she remembered his shoes. They didn't fit in with what little she'd seen, and she'd been trained to observe and analyze what didn't belong. The Senegalese were watching her as they delivered the first pallet into the hangar—apparently the driver was the one that worked here and the second was simply a friend keeping him company. But they were predictable. She'd had the same experience in many countries, though rarely so blatant. India was the worst. There the men stared at her body with dark looks of unremitting lust, never saying a word.

She looked again at the blond man.

Shoes.

Rubber-soled leather shoes like a Secret Service agent typically wore.

In Senegal.

"Agent Harley Davis?" she asked.

He looked up from befriending Iron. "Welcome to the game, Agent Sturgis."

Harley both was and wasn't what she'd pictured after reading so many of his reports. There was an anal-retentive thoroughness to them that had made her job much easier, but there had also been a casual style to the language that made them less of a chore to read than the painfully dry standard that most agents embraced. She'd imagined a short nerdy slob, not the at-ease attractively athletic man currently playing with her dog.

3

"BREAKFAST," AND HARLEY DAVIS STOOD ABRUPTLY AND walked away with the same self-assuredness that the Senegalese men had shown.

A peripheral-vision glance showed that, standing alone, she once more had the locals' undivided attention.

With a growl more befitting Iron than herself, she followed in Harley's wake.

The passage through airport security was painless as they were outbound from a military airfield. Customs non-existent.

"Should I declare my weapon?" It was buried in her pack, unloaded, but it was there.

"To who?" Harley waved toward the untended exit door. Maybe this airport wasn't as secure as she thought. No security cameras in sight either. There was a guard at the vehicle gate, in uniform, armed with a rifle, and chatting with a couple of people who appeared to be friends in no hurry to be elsewhere. Her and Harley's departure was noted with a friendly nod.

The C-130 had landed at the Dakar-Ouakam military airfield at Senghor Airport in the center of Dakar. Several years before, a new municipal airport had been built fifty kilometers out into the arid Sahel. But this old city-center base location was perhaps the best choice she'd ever seen for Air Force One. The airport was easily securable and now very underutilized, yet the city was immediately accessible to all sides.

The lack of heavy commercial traffic meant that the rest of the planes and helos that followed the President around the world wouldn't be a problem. Often they had to land, unload, and then depart to airfields elsewhere. Here they could have a whole side of the airport to themselves without crowding anybody. And the emergency backup E-4B Nightwatch command post could be placed at the other airport, giving the President two fast lines of retreat.

Step One of the security requirements. Check.

Nancy was *not* ready for the dust of the streets. It drifted over the sides of the streets in lumpy waves cluttered with cast-offs of plastic and dead flip-flops. That, she noted, was the standard footwear of the people swirling about them.

Not a New York-level crowd, but a steady stream of people. The men's attire was one of the two versions she'd seen at the airport. The women wore dresses in intense patterns of brilliant colors. Some with headwraps, some without. A flock of teenage girls in white tops and dark blue skirts rushed along clutching armfuls of textbooks and giggling together exactly like teenage girls in other countries.

Most of the people walked along in that comfortable middle ground between lazy and hustling. They had places to go but didn't appear stressed about getting there.

But she had less problem weaving through the crowds than Harley did.

"It's not you, it's Iron. Dogs aren't pets here; they're guard dogs. They're moving aside in case Iron is dangerous." Sure enough, Harley's explanation fit. People were casual even polite about it, but vendors and pedestrians alike gave Iron a wide berth.

The noise level of the city was both above and below average. Yes, there was a two-lane flow of traffic, moving along in fits and starts, but never with the roar of a major Western city. Here the major background noise was people. They talked loudly in groups, vendors called out but rather than hawking wares, they appeared to be greeting each passing friend.

Walking on the streets themselves was out of the question. Taxis, alternately racing but then slowing without warning, were mostly aging Toyota Corollas. They accounted for over half of the traffic. In the first block she spotted three more distinct transit systems. There were small vans with the classic bus boys as she'd seen in so many countries, trying to entice riders aboard. Rusty white buses, that she might have ridden to school twenty years before, were packed standing-room-only solid. And then a bus painted red and covered with wild graffiti that would have fit right into a 1960's hippie fest rumbled by.

"Most popular form of transport," Harley nodded

toward the red bus. "It symbolizes their identity in some way."

She wondered how many followed programmed routes and how many simply wandered the city, their routes determined by the accumulation of who had boarded. She'd run into both variations plenty of times.

An orangish taxi—at least it might have been orange under all of the red dust—pulled up beside them.

"Ride. Good ride. Very cheap." The driver called out his window.

"No thanks." She noted that Harley didn't make eye contact, neither did she.

But the driver didn't believe them and continued to idle alongside. "Go where you need go. Airport? Goree?" He kept listing suggestions in between *Very cheaps*.

"No form of *jalan jalan?*" she asked Harley.

Harley sighed, "Not that I've found."

In Indonesia, the *bemo* drivers were very insistent that she climb onto their van until she said *jalan jalan*—going for the sake of going. Once they understood, they'd smile in thanks for their time saved and cruise away seeking the next fare. Everywhere needed a phrase for *Going nowhere in particular, not in a hurry, and at my own pace.*

The taxi driver only gave up when he almost rear-ended a small delivery truck parked in the lane and blocking half the road.

"What's the foreigner markup?" she asked Harley.

"Factor of ten to start."

Nancy whistled. That was seriously steep.

"Basic barter can knock that down to four or five times the locals' rate. You can be here for years, but if you're white, you won't get below twice the local's rate. Which is why they're so eager to pick us up."

"Local food here isn't exactly exciting for breakfast. Plenty of American or French if you prefer."

"I didn't come to Senegal to eat at McDonald's."

This wasn't the Harley Davis she'd met in his reports. That man had a quirky sense of humor. The reports themselves were strictly professional in tone, mostly. But there was an agent-to-agent Notes section that didn't get filed up the line. The first one had said, *Guatemala, Panajachel, bring earplugs to sleep because the feral dogs are very loud at night.*

She'd replied that having a switch installed on her auditory nerves might have been a better suggestion. The dogs had decided to spend the night partying outside her room's first-floor balcony.

It had grown from there.

Last month's report on the Philippines had warned her to walk with a stoop because she'd be taller than most men, and she wouldn't want to give them an inferiority complex. At five-eight, she was taller by four inches. He'd further suggested that perhaps her dog could be taught to stoop as well to avoid embarrassing the national favorite Shih Tzus.

Senegal's Notes section had warned her that when the Sahel winds were blowing, it would be good training for her next mission to Mars: all-encompassing unbelievably fine and penetrating red dust.

This real-life Harley could be replaced with a talking lump, and he'd be about as warm.

He turned in at a small shop at the same moment

they passed the other side of the delivery truck. The taxi was waiting to pounce, then its driver grimaced at their turning aside.

The shop was smaller than her studio apartment in DC, which was not a compliment. Last year she'd booked three hundred and four days on the road. She hadn't wasted money on paying for *home* space.

At first, she thought it might be a high-crime area despite Senegal's peaceful reputation. The three of them filled up most of the shop's free space. To either side was rusted wire mesh reaching floor-to-ceiling and in front was a counter, though it didn't have the heavy wire. Goods were stacked floor-to-ceiling everywhere in the shop.

And that's when she figured out that the wire mesh was simply the back of heavily laden shelves so that the customer could see what was stacked there and it wouldn't fall on them by accident. A surprising variety of product was packed in the small space, and everything asked for was hand-picked by the merchant.

Harley rattled off some rapid French, not one of her languages. Senegal used Wolof for living, French for business, and a smattering of English according to Harley's advance report. She had the smattering of English covered.

On his small counter, the merchant pulled out a long French baguette, sliced it open, smeared on a thick layer of Nutella, then handed it over. Harley ripped it in two and handed her half. More French, and she was holding a liter box of juice with bright pink-and-red flowers on the package.

"Bissap. Made from Hibiscus flowers. It's quite good. This is the fancy version of breakfast. The basic version doesn't include the bissap juice." Then Mr. Mansplainer Harley looked down at Iron and, for the first time, appeared at a loss.

Finally.

She wiggled Iron's pack which was now hooked awkwardly over her elbow. "I have his food. But we need water."

A tall two-liter bottle of water was produced, and then Harley pulled out a wad of local money.

Crap! He'd screwed up all of her routine new-place practices. She hadn't changed any money at the airport before he'd whisked her away. Of course she'd probably have to have *married* someone to make the exchange. No sign of an ATM, or any other electronics in the entire shop. The only electrical appliances at all were an aged glass-front Coca-Cola cooler mostly filled with packets of yogurt, and a fan that rattled badly, which was aimed at the clerk.

Until she found an ATM, she was beholden to Harley as assuredly as she would be to the forklift driver if she'd agreed to marry him.

After dodging across the road, he led her to the only big tree on the entire street. Beneath it stood a ragged collection of plastic chairs.

"It's okay if we sit here." He nodded toward the wall behind him. "A couple of musicians live here, and often play under this tree in the afternoon. We'll also leave your pack with them; it'll be perfectly safe."

She sat, clamped the crisp baguette in her teeth, and

fished out Iron's double Fold-a-bowl. Half a liter of water and a cup of kibble and at least her dog was happy.

4

NANCY HAD NEVER BEEN UNCOMFORTABLE WITH SILENCE, which was one of the reasons she'd gone for the position of Advance Scout. Other than the business of local security, she often didn't talk to people for days.

Agent Harley Davis appeared to share that, when he wasn't busy mansplaining. Breakfast passed in an easy silence until Iron lay in the dirt and all she had left were a few sips of the sweet bissap juice.

"So, Harley, what are you still doing in Senegal? Shouldn't you already be out ahead of us to Morocco or Egypt by now?"

He shrugged. "I was told to meet you. This is the longest I've sat still in ages—almost two whole days. No complaints, I like Dakar. On the hustle, they have to be to make it all work, but not hyper intense like Nigeria or Ghana."

"Mellow Portland, Oregon. Not hyper Seattle or LA."

"Exactly."

She liked that the cultural references were so easy

with Harley. Few people covered the ground like a Secret Service Advance scout. The world was a part of their language.

Yet they'd overlapped. That had never happened before. Had some bean counter back in DC looked at what they each did and decided to economize them into a single person?

Nancy jolted up in her seat.

"Am I done?" The last thing she wanted to do was go back to walking the White House fence line so that Iron could sniff to see who among the gawkers might have recently been mixing explosives.

"No. Sorry, didn't mean to spook you. I'm logistics and you're security, they need both of us. However, it's a couple-day visit. The President does that so rarely that I guess they want us to double down. Because of this big conference, it's a great way for him to meet individually with many African leaders in a short time span. And it's up to us to cover the maximum amount of ground to prepare for such a long visit."

She vacillated between relieved and annoyed. The first because she would still be doing the job she loved. But was she now to be paired with this humorless mansplainer?

Not so much.

5

Nancy had very little time to feel put out by that.

They visited the African Renaissance Monument, a sixteen-story-tall bronze statue of a man holding aloft his child, while drawing his scantily clad wife along in his wake. Harley probably loved the image.

It was perched atop one of the only two hills in Dakar. The second was some seven hundred meters away and sported a large lighthouse at the peak. The lighthouse would need to be secured but would also be a good outpost for a Delta Force overwatch sniper team during a visit to the monument.

If the city was hot, climbing to the base of the monument, up the two hundred and four gritty concrete steps, was eviscerating. The President would have an easier time of it in the Spring. Thank God there was an elevator to the top of the monument itself. No more than six people could fit into the circular lift at a time and, when they reached the top, she saw why.

The elevator door opened into the center of a small

space apparently high inside the male's head. The first window she looked out of elicited a yelp of surprise. Her reaction caused a suspicious growl and a quick scan for threats from Iron.

"What is it?" Harley twisted around to look at her.

"Sorry. False alarm, girl," she stroked Iron's head. She pointed out and down at the gigantic woman's face looking directly up at her. Her eyes looked alien up close. And her face... "She doesn't look Senegalese."

"Nope," Harley said complacently. "It's one of many, many complaints about this monument. The cost. The scantily clad woman lording much of her butt over a heavily Muslim country. The fact that the three caricatures have distinctly Korean features. Building massive bronze statues in African countries is one of the few forms of trade still allowed for North Korea other than cybercrime. The catch is, they always look Korean, not African."

She stared down at the woman's face a moment longer and then turned to look at the sweep of the city. Packed tightly into a large triangular peninsula, the Atlantic Ocean surrounded the city on all sides. With the red Sahel dust filling the skies, the farther limits of the urban sprawl faded with the visibility of five miles. When the President was here next Spring, the view should be magnificent.

They spent most of an hour, working their way around the glass windows, identifying the various locations that the President's handlers had identified as being of interest.

"The First Lady will enjoy visiting the two botanic

gardens." Though Nancy had not met her, she'd studied Anne Darlington carefully. She often traveled with the President but had very different priorities. She was a leader in the Farm to Table and Slow Food movements. The chance to visit a foreign botanic garden would be at the top of her list as she was very active on the board of DC's own.

"The President will want to join her for the trip out to the garden on Goree Island. It's one of those must-visit locales. From there, half a million slaves were shipped out of West Africa to the Americas and Caribbean Islands."

Nancy gave a shiver. Reading the reports, then seeing it perched there offshore in the blue sea reflecting the red sky was something else again.

It was a low city, two- and three-story buildings dominated, four-to-six existed but there were no skyscrapers. The two hills, including the monument on top, would disappear in cities like New York or Tokyo. She stood at the very pinnacle, barely forty-five stories above the sea.

6

HARLEY SLOWLY THAWED THROUGHOUT THE DAY...AT LEAST with Iron. Herself? He was still Mr. Mansplainer Stiff-neck.

They visited mosques and a pickup soccer game on a dusty, dirt lot.

They toured the conference site twenty kilometers out from the city, an unlikely modern building with large expanses of glass and an unexpected green lawn. It was unlike anything else in the whole beige city. The grass was so green that it looked fresh washed. In the arid semi-desert, vast shallow pools of water wrapped around two sides of the complex. Yet not fifty meters away stood a massive baobab in the scrubland. A tall gray pillar too fat to be a tree, but it had a scraggle of branches at the top to prove it was.

They met with a very efficient head of security.

Having Iron along was very illustrative. She had a good instinct for what could be a security challenge regarding explosives. As Nancy guided her through each inspection, she also identified the level of triggers they would have to worry about.

The conference center's main security office was a major trigger, of course. There were too many weapons and rounds, which created a veritable perfumed cloud of gunpowder residues. Though the Secret Service would have numerous agents deeply embedded there anyway, it was worth noting. But the rest of the center was very clean: scent-wise and physically.

Iron also triggered on the spent powder of one officer who had come fresh from the shooting range. Nancy made the usual note that all native security personnel must be told to wear clothes laundered after their latest range practice before the Presidential visit. Otherwise every sniffer dog in the entourage would be alerting to the spent gunpowder on their sleeves.

Senegalese poaching was mostly about illegal overfishing, not hunters of ivory or rare pelts. There were no scents from gunfire there to worry about either.

Lunch was on the fly and by the time they'd returned to the heart of the city, Nancy was grinding to a halt. Iron had slept on the flight over, but she hadn't.

Harley had the taxi drop them along a narrow strip of steep, rocky beach as the sun descended toward the watery horizon of the Atlantic.

"I need food and sleep at this point. Not some pretty little sunset."

"This *is* the food part," Harley explained without, for once, explaining too much.

He led her past a cliff-side restaurant and down a set of uneven stone steps.

At the beach, he took off his shoes.

"I'm not going for a swim."

"No, but I thought Iron might appreciate it." He waved to the south. A little way along, a tall Senegalese man had led a large German Shepherd into the surf at the end of a heavy hank of rope. The dog had a gimp leg, which made him unsteady in the surf. He didn't like the waves at all and tried to huddle on the sandy patches as they swirled around the boulders. But he tolerated it as the man scrubbed water into his fur.

"Saltwater helps with ticks and skin irritation. It also cools him off. That's Cora and Clovis. I met them here yesterday. His family lives by that big tree where we had breakfast. They're having the *grillade* here tomorrow, grilled fish and vegetables on rice. We've been invited. They're a very social culture, very big on inclusion."

Harley and Cora traded waves but apparently that was sufficient interaction as the man returned his attention to bathing his dog.

It *was* cooler here. The waves breaking on the rocks provided some moisture to the parched air.

And Iron did love to swim.

No sticks to throw. She'd seen very little wood of any kind except for the occasional dusty baobab tree looking as if it was holding up the sky.

She unsnapped Iron's leash. Iron was too well trained to need it, but the locals had definitely appreciated it.

Nancy waved her toward the water. She hopped onto a larger rock, then plunged in with a leap that sent a wide spray over Harley where he stood with one shoe on and one off.

She laughed as he spluttered.

For the first time all day she could stop worrying about the rate of Iron's panting.

She turned to watch Iron paddling about happily in the low surf. She snapped at a wave, shook her head shedding a spray of water, and began to swim for shore. Nothing else coming to hand, Nancy picked up a rock and heaved it out to sea.

Iron twisted about and raced through the waves toward where it had disappeared. She looked about, expecting to see a tennis ball floating on the surface. Iron didn't fall for it when Nancy tried the trick a second time. Instead, Nancy dug a tennis ball out of Iron's pack, which she'd carried herself all day, and tossed it for her dog.

She raced to it, snagging it in mid-stroke, and zoomed to shore. She brought it to Nancy, handed it over, then raced back to the waterline, before turning to watch her eagerly.

Nancy paused a few extra seconds and Iron gave a great shake, spraying yet more water on Harley.

"Feels good," he laughed as she heaved the ball again and Iron dove off his rock, leapt over the next wave before plunging in.

"I didn't know you could laugh in addition to all of your, uh, explaining."

"Is that how you've been seeing me all day? A humorless idiot with a need to explain everything?"

"Well, you haven't shown much of the humor that's in your reports, and you specialize in the latter."

Harley looked puzzled at that. "I like understanding what's going on. And I thought... Never mind."

7

Harley walked abruptly away, still carrying one sock and shoe while wearing the other.

Iron was still playing in the surf, tossing the ball aside herself, ducking under a wave, and surprising it from underneath like a black furry shark. She'd been so good all day that Nancy didn't want to cut off this fun.

Somehow the Secret Service agent, named after a motorcycle, having actual feelings wasn't something she'd expected. Nancy kept an eye on his progress as he reclimbed the stone steps to the restaurant, pausing halfway up to put on his shoe.

The sun had set, and the abrupt equatorial dark was descending by the time Iron was ready to come back ashore.

With a quick command, Nancy kept her at a distance until she'd shaken the water from her coat several times.

Then they headed up the stairs in search of Harley, trying to figure out how to apologize for telling the truth. Too abruptly, of course. At least that fit.

"I'm far too used to being on my own," she told Iron when they were about halfway up to the restaurant.

"I know that problem all too well."

She startled when Harley's voice sounded from the dark.

"You could have warned me," she whispered to Iron, who ignored her and trotted over to greet him like a long-lost friend—or at least a long-lost ear scritcher.

The light trickling down from the restaurant, combined with the dust-red crescent moon and the very last of the bloody sunset, lit a sandy terrace beside the path enough to reveal vague shapes. Held in place by a low ridge of stone, the sandy patch boasted a thatch-roof hut with open sides, and a couple of chairs.

"Tomorrow night, if we're still here, my musician friends are going to have a traditional feed right here, that *grillade* I mentioned—a grilling of fish and veggies over rice and sauce. Tonight, I've asked the restaurant to provide us dinner. They cook Italian, I hope that's okay. I asked them for their two specials and you can pick. They'll also bring down some burger for Iron. And I'm overexplaining everything again, aren't I?"

She was too tired to do more than be thankful for him taking care of dinner. She'd rather hoped that Harley would be taking off before tomorrow, though having a personal guide around the city had been very efficient. And he was pleasant enough. But—

"Why are you always so stiff around me?" she asked as the three of them settled to watch the brighter stars battling their way out. They seemed a shade brighter with each wave that rolled onto the beach below.

"Hmm... Because your dog has more common sense than I do?"

"Well, Iron has a great deal of common sense."

"So I've noticed. Why did you name her Iron?"

Nancy started to give her standard answer, that her labradoodle's coat was an atypical iron gray. Instead, as a sort of apology for what she'd said earlier, she told him the truth. It was something she never told anyone.

"She's named Iron because she came after me."

"Nancy Iron Sturgis?"

"No, she isn't *named* after me. She's what came the night after— Crap!" She rubbed at her gritty eyes. "It doesn't make sense when I try to explain when I'm *not* sleep deprived. Right now, I'm a mess. Okay, have you heard of Sturgis? The motorcycle rally?"

"Hello. I'm named for my parents' motorcycle. There's some icky family story about the first time they made love it was while straddling..." Harley's silhouette shuddered. "How sad is that?"

"Well, I'm a direct descendant of General Samuel D. Sturgis, about six generations out. He's the one who the South Dakota city is named after, which the motorcycle rally of half-a-million people is named after *in turn*. And the year I was conceived—I can't believe I'm saying this— I was conceived at a Nancy Sinatra concert at the rally. Or perhaps the next night at the Iron Butterfly concert. So, I became Nancy...and named *her,*" she patted her dog's head, "Iron. She came *after* me."

"So, you could have been named 'In-A-Gadda-Da-Vida'."

"Sure, that's my middle name, didn't you know?"

"Motorcycle man, motorcycle gal, and motorcycle dog."

"Iron doesn't like motorcycles. She thinks they're made by space aliens."

"It's the only good form of transport on Mars. Cars keep getting bogged down in the red dust."

"There you are!" Nancy felt a little bit as if she was pouncing. "Where the hell have *you* been all day, Harley?"

He grunted uncertainly, as a waiter brought down two platters. He offered her mushroom chicken on vermicelli pasta or a *Frutti di Mare* on fettuccini.

She took the Fruit of the Sea platter; Italian *was* one of her languages and definitely her favorite cuisine. Of course, it was Senegalese seafood, so she wondered how much would be familiar. The lush smells said she wouldn't care.

The waiter also set a plate of raw beef in front of Iron, which disappeared within seconds of arrival.

8

———

THEY'D EATEN IN SILENCE, ENJOYING THE GOOD FOOD AND the cooling of the day...except for her feet, which were baking because Iron had once again fallen asleep on them, pinning them in place.

"I guess I do always do that." Harley wasn't even a shadow in the darkness anymore.

"Do what?" If there was still a thread to their conversation, she'd lost it long ago.

"Explain things."

"I'm getting used to that. I have this new theory that you're not innately obnoxious, you're just one of those people who loves knowledge *for its own sake.*"

"I am. Aren't you?" Harley's voice sounded shocked, and not all in mock disbelief.

Nancy had to think about that as she wedged her feet out from under Iron and rested them on her belly. "No, I don't think so."

In retrospect, she realized that it was one of the things she'd liked most about Harley's reports. Everything was always explained clearly. She didn't know why it bothered her in person. Maybe it hadn't. Maybe it was simply the in-personness of him that had been more in her face than expected. Having a fellow agent around was also being something of a mind bender.

"I'm, perhaps, far too used to being alone with my dog. Living with a dog is a very Be Here Now, present-tense kind of thinking. I often think that if I had a dog translator, Iron's every other word would be Now? Now? How about now?"

It earned her a small laugh. "I'm, perhaps, far too sick of being alone."

"Really? But, Harley, you've chosen one of the most isolating, rootless careers there is within the Secret Service. Like well-paid hobo or something."

"I'd have long since asked for reassignment if it wasn't for you."

"Me?" She wished she could see Harley's expression.

"You're the first person who ever responded to my scouting reports past *Received*. You can't have any idea what a difference that makes."

She too had always felt as if they were having a long-distance conversation. Nancy recalled one report in which he'd complained about logistics for the Marine One helicopters and how it would be easier if they didn't have rotors when attempting to land at a Japanese temple sanctuary—but instead had silent, anti-gravity pods. She'd always been rather proud of her own response that there could be a problem with stray Buddhas accidentally ascending to heaven when caught in the anti-gravity field on departure.

"I liked our...conversations." She wasn't sure what else to call them, because they had felt like more than that.

"Our...flirting?"

Was that what they'd been doing? She turned to study Harley's dim profile. He was staring out to sea —*studiously* staring out to sea. Had he known all along that's what they were doing? If so, she could certainly do with a little mansplaining right about now.

"Harley?"

"Uh-huh?"

"Are..." But she didn't know what to ask.

Then she was, literally saved by the bell when both of their phones rang.

Relief? Or disappointment?

She wasn't sure.

9

NANCY COULD SEE BY HARLEY'S SHIFTING POSITION IN HIS chair that he was being told the same thing she was by another Secret Service operator who had no way to know they sat only three feet apart.

Death of one of the First Lady's closest friends. Funeral in Lerwick, Shetland Islands, UK, in forty-eight hours. Flight out of Blaise Diagne International Airport in one hour.

That was a problem. That wasn't the military airport in town, it was the new commercial airport, located fifty kilometers out the far side of Dakar. They were both on their feet and moving before the call was done. They grabbed their plates and raced up to the restaurant while they were still on their phones.

"One hour?" she asked Harley as he paid the restaurateur. The new airport was near-enough an hour away by taxi.

"Tight. But we've got it."

She'd been worried about finding a taxi. They could

be impossible to find in New York or DC, where, like Dakar, most of the transport was by cab. She shouldn't have. The moment they reached the road, a taxi pulled up.

"Airport? Hotel? My brother have very nice rooms. Very cheap!"

They retrieved their packs from the house by the gathering tree. But insisting they were in a hurry didn't get them away quickly. First, she had to meet everybody, which included a great deal of handshaking. After a puzzling round of congratulations—all to Harley, she noted—she figured out what was going on and explained that they weren't a couple. That mistake delayed them further and earned a number of interested glances that they were polite enough not to voice. Which saved her siccing Iron on them. Which *was* overreacting. Where was a Corgi when she desperately needed a group of men herded in another direction—*any* other direction.

Then the realization that they'd be missing tomorrow's *grillade* was an issue of some discussion in rapid French. After that, the length of the drive across Dakar to meet the night flight to Heathrow became a topic of hot debate. It didn't seem to matter that the debate itself was slicing more deeply into their time with each passing sentence.

Next, the cabbie joined in using some other language. He left his car to block an entire lane of traffic in front of the house and added his own opinions to the others.

Harley pulled out his phone. Somehow, he had a conversation in the middle of a debate that was making her head ache as everyone seemed to be speaking at once.

He hung up, "Okay, we're good to go."

Wise enough to not offer an explanation for once, which would open up to yet more consideration, they were swiftly ushered back into the cab.

Minutes later they were once more at the military airport where her morning had begun so long ago. The C-130 transport that had delivered her was nowhere in sight. Thankfully, neither was the forklift driver. An ancient Russian Mil Mi-2 helicopter, painted the bright white of the Senegalese Air Force, was warming up outside one of the hangars.

"You *are* Mr. Logistics."

Harley offered a radiant smile as the two of them, with Iron trotting alongside, hurried over to the helo. "The Senegalese President offered the Air Force's assistance as part of the site prep team when the time comes. Consider this a dry run."

Fifteen minutes later they were across Dakar and a fifty-kilometer stretch of arid semi-desert, landing near the British Airways commercial jet. No customs. No exit stamps. Off the helo and onto the plane. Thankfully, in the rush of being last aboard, the stewards ushered Iron straight aboard with them.

At the very rear of the plane, Iron claimed the window seat. Harley's long legs claimed the aisle. She collapsed between them.

Nancy woke briefly when the tires squealed on the runway. She vaguely remembered the transfer and only truly awoke when they land in Inverness, Scotland.

By the crick in her neck, she'd spent both flights passed out on Harley's shoulder.

By his grin, he'd enjoyed every second of it.

10

EIGHT HOURS OF SLEEP IN-FLIGHT DIDN'T REPLACE TWO days awake, but it certainly helped.

It was also the last sleep they were to have over the next three days. Even her indefatigable labradoodle, who had slept every time they were in a car or meeting, was dragging by the end of it.

But they were the United States Secret Service and they got it done.

From Inverness, they'd hustled out to Royal Air Force Base Lossiemouth. It was the farthest north airport that could comfortably accommodate Air Force One, the Marine One helos, and the massive and massively heavy C-5 Galaxy transport jets that had ferried the helos and the Motorcade across the Atlantic. An expedited booking placed the Motorcade onto tomorrow's Aberdeen-Lerwick ferry for the twelve-hour crossing to the Shetland Islands so that its vehicles would arrive in town with hours to spare.

When everything escalated because the President had decided to accompany his wife, they took it in stride.

After coordinating with RAF Lossiemouth and the Aberdeen ferry, they flew out to Lerwick.

On their accelerated timeline, they departed northern Scotland fifteen minutes ahead of the first wave of the main team's arrival.

Only by moving at a dead run were they able to keep that lead as they coordinated with the Lerwick Police, the Shetland Museum regarding a possible visit, and even Jamieson & Smith Wool Brokers about a personal tour because the First Lady was an avid knitter.

Her friend's estate house—where the funeral, burial in the family lot, and wake were to be held—was the last area to be fully scouted.

They'd been constantly feeding their assessments back up the chain of command. Staffing was adjusted downward in some places, up in others. Marine One would be the prime transport outside of Lerwick, but the Motorcade was an essential element within the small town. However, the Motorcade itself had to be downsized otherwise the normal thirty-vehicle cavalcade that accompanied the President would lock the town up from one end to the other.

This was a private visit rather than a State one, which cut the overall operation's scale dramatically. And the word from the estate owner that, "Of course, Zachary and Anne will be staying with us," saved the trouble of having to locate and sufficiently secure an additional hotel site.

They exited out the back of the estate seven full

minutes ahead of the scheduled arrival of the lead security team.

The estate owner pointed at the garden path. "Lovely walk, that way. Follow the shore of the loch along the paved path. It will bring you right around, past the broch, and into the other side of town."

Nancy knew a *loch* was a lake, and she figured they'd know a *broch* when they saw one. As always, she was glad to escape before the big security teams arrived.

11

Nancy could feel the last seventy-two hours sliding off her shoulders as she, Iron, and Harley walked along the lake shore. Lushly green, a brilliant sky above because it was one of those rare, perfectly clear days in the Shetlands; it felt so alive.

So did she.

She glanced down at Iron who was happily zigzagging from the lake shore to the towering rhododendron bushes that carpeted the hillside. Across the lake on a small peninsula stood a circular stone structure a story or so high.

"That must be a *broch*."

"Must be," Harley spoke softly as he strolled close beside her.

She waited. But... "What, no explanation?"

"I was trying to restrain myself."

Nancy considered, listened to how she felt. To be strolling along with the only other person she'd ever met who understood both the joys and pains of being alone in the same way she did was...nice—*very* nice. She whispered, "Don't."

"Well," Harley clapped his hands together like the excited ten-year-old who lurked not far beneath his skin. "The *Broch of Clickimin* was constructed in about four hundred BC and shows a characteristic hollow wall, two close-laid stone walls with a space between, that was apparently designed specifically to offer future archeologists and architects an extremely obscure topic to disagree about at length over bowls of steaming punch."

"It's too nice a day for a bowl of steaming punch."

"How about a pint of ale at the pub with a side of bangers and mash?"

"With you?"

Harley grinned, "That was the idea."

Nancy watched the triangle formed by the sides of the loch. The town to the east, the estate to the north and west, and the *broch* to the south. "I had another idea."

"Better than ale, bangers, and mash? You know that Iron Butterfly is a big fan of bangers." Harley found a stick and tossed it ahead for Iron.

"I know that."

What Nancy didn't quite know was if she was ready for the idea that had fallen on her head.

"I'm so far past exhaustion that perhaps I'm in a higher state of consciousness. It certainly seems clear from up here, wherever this is," she told him as Iron returned the stick and Harley pitched it again.

"Scotland," Harley informed her in a serious tone. "We're in Scotland."

"Don't say that to a Shetlander. Besides, are you sure this isn't Mars?"

"No, not Mars. No red, gritty dust storms. Scotland, not Mars."

Nancy scoffed as they circled the bottom of the *loch* and stood before the remains of the *broch* built twenty-five centuries ago.

"So what's this grand vision from on high?" Harley asked.

She glanced briefly at him but decided she'd be better off looking away. Then she looked down at Iron, but her labradoodle was busy having her head rubbed by Harley.

"Well, we're all motorcycle people. Seems to me that riding together has worked pretty damn well so far."

Harley stopped scratching Iron's ear and gave her his full attention.

She did her best to give her full attention to a twenty-five-hundred-year-old pile of stone that definitely was *not* a security risk. It wasn't working.

But he didn't speak, leaving it up to her to do the explaining this time.

"Instead of Advance *Scouts,* doesn't it seem more effective to do logistics and security together? You know, as an Advance *Team.*"

"But DC—"

"The coordinators back in DC aren't out here, they wouldn't know what's best. We do."

"Team as in three?" Harley asked slowly.

It no longer sounded quite so clairvoyant. But she *liked* Harley. Even more than she'd expected from his reports, and far more than his ever-so-overly careful first impression in person.

And from up *there,* in her fast-fogging vision, she'd thought maybe he'd been all strange when they finally met in Dakar because he liked her. And... Her brain was about to loop around on itself so fast that, like the big atom collider in Switzerland, her synapses were going to fuse.

Then Harley slid his hand into hers and it became the only thing she could feel in the whole world. All sensation seemed to be focused on the slightest touch of their fingers sliding together as if they'd always been that way.

"I could get to like that idea."

"More than Mars?" Her voice was barely a whisper on the Scottish air.

"More than the stars."

"That is big, isn't it?"

Harley nodded as he smiled down at her.

Maybe the idea of making an Advance Team of two— Iron nudged their joined hands with her cold nose—of three, *was* that big.

"You know this is actually Iron's team, right?"

Harley smiled at her, "Well, duh!"

He didn't have to explain a thing.

OFF THE LEASH (EXCERPT)

IF YOU ENJOYED THAT, YOU'LL LOVE THE NOVELS!

OFF THE LEASH (EXCERPT)

"You're joking."

"Nope. That's his name. And he's yours now."

Sergeant Linda Hamlin wondered quite what it would take to wipe that smile off Lieutenant Jurgen's face. A 120mm round from an M1A1 Abrams Main Battle Tank came to mind.

The kennel master of the US Secret Service's Canine Team was clearly a misogynistic jerk from the top of his polished head to the bottoms of his equally polished boots. She wondered if the shoelaces were polished as well.

Then she looked over at the poor dog sitting hopefully on the concrete kennel floor. His stall had a dog bed three times his size and a water bowl deep enough for him to bathe in. No toys, because toys always came from the handler as a reward. He offered her a sad sigh and a liquid doggy gaze. The kennel even smelled wrong, more of sanitizer than dog. The walls seemed to echo with each bark down the long line of kennels housing the candidate hopefuls for the next addition to the Secret Service's team.

Thor—really?—was a brindle-colored mutt, part who-knew and part no-one-cared. He looked like a cross between an oversized, long-haired schnauzer and a dust mop that someone had spilled dark gray paint on. After mixing in streaks of tawny brown, they'd left one white paw just to make him all the more laughable.

And of course Lieutenant Jerk Jurgen would assign Thor to the first woman on the USSS K-9 team.

Unable to resist, she leaned over far enough to scruff the dog's ears. He was the physical opposite of the sleek and powerful Malinois MWDs—military war dogs—that she'd been handling for the 75th Rangers for the last five years. They twitched with eagerness and nerves. A good MWD was seventy pounds of pure drive—every damn second of the day. If the mild-mannered Thor weighed thirty pounds, she'd be surprised. And he looked like a little girl's best friend who should have a pink bow on his collar.

Jurgen was clearly ex-Marine and would have no respect for the Army. Of course, having been in the Army's Special Operations Forces, she knew better than to respect a Marine.

"We won't let any old swabbie bother us, will we?"

Jurgen snarled—definitely Marine Corps. Swabbie was slang for a Navy sailor and a Marine always took offense at being lumped in with them no matter how much they belonged. Of course the swabbies took offense at having the Marines lumped with *them*. Too bad there weren't any Navy around so that she could get two for the price of one. Jurgen wouldn't be her boss, so appeasing him wasn't high on her to-do list.

At least she wouldn't need any of the protective bite gear working with Thor. With his stature, he was an explosives detection dog without also being an attack one.

"Where was he trained?" She stood back up to face the beast.

"Private outfit in Montana—some place called Henderson's Ranch. Didn't make their MWD program," his scoff said exactly what he thought the likelihood of any dog outfit in Montana being worthwhile. "They wanted us to try the little runt out."

She'd never heard of a training program in Montana. MWDs all came out of Lackland Air Force Base training. The Secret Service mostly trained their own and they all came from Vohne Liche Kennels in Indiana. Unless... Special Operations Forces dogs were trained by private contractors. She'd worked beside a Delta Force dog for a single month—he'd been incredible.

"Is he trained in English or German?" Most American MWDs were trained in German so that there was no confusion in case a command word happened to be part of a spoken sentence. It also made it harder for any random person on the battlefield to shout something that would confuse the dog.

"German according to his paperwork, but he won't listen to me much in either language."

Might as well give the diminutive Thor a few basic tests. A snap of her fingers and a slap on her thigh had the dog dropping into a smart "heel" position. No need to call out *Fuss*—*by my foot.*

"*Pass auf!*" *Guard!* She made a pistol with her thumb and forefinger and aimed it at Jurgen as she grabbed her forearm with her other hand—the military hand sign for enemy.

The little dog snarled at Jurgen sharply enough to have him backing out of the kennel. "Goddamn it!"

"*Ruhig.*" *Quiet.* Thor maintained his fierce posture but dropped the snarl.

"*Gute Hund.*" *Good dog,* Linda countered the command.

Thor looked up at her and wagged his tail happily. She tossed him a doggie treat, which he caught midair and crunched happily.

She didn't bother looking up at Jurgen as she knelt once more to check over the little dog. His scruffy fur was so soft that it tickled. Good strength in the jaw, enough to show he'd had bite training despite his size—perfect if she ever needed to take down a three-foot-tall terrorist. Legs said he was a jumper.

"Take your time, Hamlin. I've got nothing else to do with the rest of my goddamn day except babysit you and this mutt."

"Is the course set?"

"Sure. Take him out," Jurgen's snarl sounded almost as nasty as Thor's before he stalked off.

She stood and slapped a hand on her opposite shoulder.

Thor sprang aloft as if he was attached to springs and she caught him easily. He'd cleared well over double his own height. Definitely trained...and far easier to catch than seventy pounds of hyperactive Malinois.

She plopped him back down on the ground. On lead or off? She'd give him the benefit of the doubt and try off first to see what happened.

Linda zipped up her brand-new USSS jacket against the cold and led the way out of the kennel into the hard sunlight of the January morning. Snow had brushed the higher hills around the USSS James J. Rowley Training Center—which this close to Washington, DC, wasn't saying much—but was melting quickly. Scents wouldn't carry as well on the cool air, making it more of a challenge for Thor to locate the explosives. She didn't know where they were either. The course was a test for handler as well as dog.

Jurgen would be up in the observer turret looking for any excuse to mark down his newest team. Perhaps teasing him about being just a Marine hadn't been her best tactical choice. She sighed. At least she was consistent—she'd always been good at finding ways to piss people off before she could stop herself and consider the wisdom of doing so.

This test was the culmination of a crazy three months, so she'd forgive herself this time—something she also wasn't very good at.

In October she'd been out of the Army and unsure what to do next. Tucked in the packet with her DD 214 honorable discharge form had been a flyer on career opportunities with the US Secret Service dog team: *Be all your dog can be!* No one else being released from Fort

Benning that day had received any kind of a job flyer at all that she'd seen, so she kept quiet about it.

She had to pass through DC on her way back to Vermont—her parent's place. Burlington would work for, honestly, not very long at all, but she lacked anywhere else to go after a decade of service. So, she'd stopped off in DC to see what was up with that job flyer. Five interviews and three months to complete a standard six-month training course later—which was mostly a cakewalk after fighting with the US Rangers—she was on-board and this chill January day was her first chance with a dog. First chance to prove that she still had it. First chance to prove that she hadn't made a mistake in deciding that she'd seen enough bloodshed and war zones for one lifetime and leaving the Army.

The Start Here sign made it obvious where to begin, but she didn't dare hesitate to take in her surroundings past a quick glimpse. Jurgen's score would count a great deal toward where she and Thor were assigned in the future. Mostly likely on some field prep team, clearing the way for presidential visits.

As usual, hindsight informed her that harassing the lieutenant hadn't been an optimal strategy. A hindsight that had served her equally poorly with regular Army commanders before she'd finally hooked up with the Rangers—kowtowing to officers had never been one of her strengths.

Thankfully, the Special Operations Forces hadn't given a damn about anything except performance and *that* she could always deliver, since the day she'd been named the team captain for both soccer and volleyball.

She was never popular, but both teams had made all-state her last two years in school.

The canine training course at James J. Rowley was a two-acre lot. A hard-packed path of tramped-down dirt led through the brown grass. It followed a predictable pattern from the gate to a junker car, over to tool shed, then a truck, and so on into a compressed version of an intersection in a small town. Beyond it ran an urban street of gray clapboard two- and three-story buildings and an eight-story office tower, all without windows. Clearly a playground for Secret Service training teams.

Her target was the town, so she blocked the city street out of her mind. Focus on the problem: two roads, twenty storefronts, six houses, vehicles, pedestrians.

It might look normal...normalish with its missing windows and no movement. It would be anything but. Stocked with fake IEDs, a bombmaker's stash, suicide cars, weapons caches, and dozens of other traps, all waiting for her and Thor to find. He had to be sensitive to hundreds of scents and it was her job to guide him so that he didn't miss the opportunity to find and evaluate each one.

There would be easy scents, from fertilizer and diesel fuel used so destructively in the 1995 Oklahoma City bombing, to almost as obvious TNT to the very difficult to detect C-4 plastic explosive.

Mannequins on the street carried grocery bags and briefcases. Some held fresh meat, a powerful smell demanding any dog's attention, but would count as a false lead if they went for it. On the job, an explosives detection dog wasn't supposed to care about anything except explosives. Other mannequins were wrapped in suicide vests loaded with Semtex or wearing knapsacks filled with package bombs made from Russian PVV-5A.

She spotted Jurgen stepping into a glassed-in observer turret atop the corner drugstore. Someone else was already there and watching.

She looked down once more at the ridiculous little dog and could only hope for the best.

"Thor?"

He looked up at her.

She pointed to the left, away from the beaten path.

"*Such!*" *Find.*

Thor sniffed left, then right. Then he headed forward quickly in the direction she pointed.

————

CLIVE ANDREWS SAT IN THE SECOND-STORY WINDOW AT THE corner of Main and First, the only two streets in town. Downstairs was a drugstore all rigged to explode, except there were no triggers and there was barely enough explosive to blow up a candy box.

Not that he'd know, but that's what Lieutenant Jurgen had promised him.

It didn't really matter if it was rigged to blow for real, because when Miss Watson—never Ms. or Mrs.—asked for a "favor," you did it. At least he did. Actually, he had yet to meet anyone else who knew her. Not that he'd asked around. She wasn't the sort of person one talked about with strangers, or even close friends. He'd bet even if they did, it would be in whispers. That's just what she was like.

So he'd traveled across town from the White House and into Maryland on a cold winter's morning, barely past a sunrise that did nothing to warm the day. Now he sat in an unheated glass icebox and watched a new officer run a test course he didn't begin to understand. Lieutenant Jurgen settled in beside him at a console with feeds from a dozen cameras and banks of switches.

While waiting, Clive had been fooling around with a sketch on a small pad of paper. The next State Dinner was in seven days. President Zachary Taylor had invited the leaders of Vietnam, Japan, and the Philippines to the White House for discussions about some Chinese islands. Or something like that, Clive hadn't really been paying attention to the details past the attendee list.

Instead, he was contemplating the dessert for such a dinner that would surprise, perhaps delight, as well as being an icebreaker for future discussions. Being the chocolatier for the White House was the most exciting job he'd ever had. Every challenge was fresh and new, like the first strawberry of each year.

This one would be elegant. January was a little early, it would be better if it was spring, but that wasn't crucial. A large half-egg shape of paper-thin white chocolate filled with a mousse—white chocolate? No, nor a dark chocolate. Instead, a milk chocolate mousse but rich with flavor, perhaps bourbon. Then mold the dark chocolate to top it with a filigree bird, wings spread in half flight, ready to soar upward. A crane perhaps? He made a note to check with the protocol office to make sure that he wouldn't be offending some leader without knowing it.

"Never underestimate the power of a good dessert," he mumbled one of Jacques Torres' favorite admonitions. This was going to work very nicely.

"What's that?" Jurgen grunted out without looking up.

"Just talking to myself."

Which earned him a dismissive grunt, as if he was unworthy of the agent's attention. It wouldn't surprise him.

———

Keep reading now!
Available at fine retailers everywhere.
Off the Leash

ABOUT THE AUTHOR

USA Today and Amazon #1 Bestseller M. L. "Matt" Buchman has 70+ action-adventure thriller and military romance novels, 100 short stories, and lotsa audiobooks. PW says: "Tom Clancy fans open to a strong female lead will clamor for more." Booklist declared: "3X Top 10 of the Year." A project manager with a geophysics degree, he's designed and built houses, flown and jumped out of planes, solo-sailed a 50' sailboat, and bicycled solo around the world...and he quilts. More at: www. mlbuchman.com.

Other works by M. L. Buchman: *(* - also in audio)*

Action-Adventure Thrillers

Dead Chef
One Chef!
Two Chef!

Miranda Chase
Drone*
Thunderbolt*
Condor*
Ghostrider*
Raider*
Chinook*
Havoc*
White Top*
Start the Chase*

Science Fiction / Fantasy

Deities Anonymous
Cookbook from Hell: Reheated
Saviors 101

Single Titles
Monk's Maze
the Me and Elsie Chronicles

Contemporary Romance

Eagle Cove
Return to Eagle Cove
Recipe for Eagle Cove
Longing for Eagle Cove
Keepsake for Eagle Cove

Love Abroad
Heart of the Cotswolds: England
Path of Love: Cinque Terre, Italy

Where Dreams
Where Dreams are Born
Where Dreams Reside
Where Dreams Are of Christmas*
Where Dreams Unfold
Where Dreams Are Written
Where Dreams Continue

Non-Fiction

Strategies for Success
Managing Your Inner Artist/Writer
Estate Planning for Authors*
Character Voice
Narrate and Record Your Own
Audiobook*

Short Story Series by M. L. Buchman:

Action-Adventure Thrillers

Dead Chef

Miranda Chase Origin Stories

Romantic Suspense

Antarctic Ice Fliers

US Coast Guard

Contemporary Romance

Eagle Cove

Other

Deities Anonymous (fantasy)

Single Titles

The Emily Beale Universe
(military romantic suspense)

The Night Stalkers
MAIN FLIGHT
The Night Is Mine
I Own the Dawn
Wait Until Dark
Take Over at Midnight
Light Up the Night
Bring On the Dusk
By Break of Day
Target of the Heart
Target Lock on Love
Target of Mine
Target of One's Own
NIGHT STALKERS HOLIDAYS
Daniel's Christmas*
Frank's Independence Day*
Peter's Christmas*
Christmas at Steel Beach
Zachary's Christmas*
Roy's Independence Day*
Damien's Christmas*
Christmas at Peleliu Cove

Henderson's Ranch
Nathan's Big Sky*
Big Sky, Loyal Heart*
Big Sky Dog Whisperer*
Tales of Henderson's Ranch*

Shadow Force: Psi
At the Slightest Sound*
At the Quietest Word*
At the Merest Glance*
At the Clearest Sensation*

White House Protection Force
Off the Leash*
On Your Mark*
In the Weeds*

Firehawks
Pure Heat
Full Blaze
Hot Point*
Flash of Fire*
Wild Fire
SMOKEJUMPERS
Wildfire at Dawn*
Wildfire at Larch Creek*
Wildfire on the Skagit*

Delta Force
Target Engaged*
Heart Strike*
Wild Justice*
Midnight Trust*

Emily Beale Universe Short Story Series
The Night Stalkers
The Night Stalkers Stories
The Night Stalkers CSAR
The Night Stalkers Wedding Stories
The Future Night Stalkers

Delta Force
Th Delta Force Shooters
The Delta Force Warriors

Firehawks
The Firehawks Lookouts
The Firehawks Hotshots
The Firebirds

White House Protection Force
Stories

Future Night Stalkers
Stories (Science Fiction)

The Emily Beale Universe
Reading Order Road Map

any series and any novel may be read stand-alone
(all have a complete heartwarming Happy Ever After)

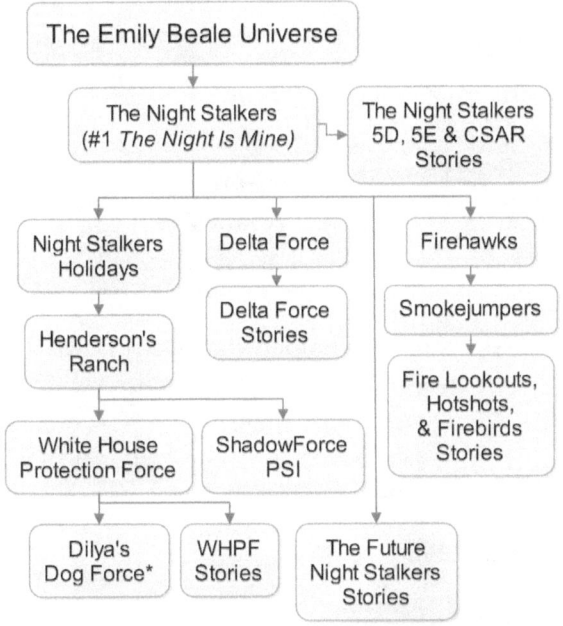

The Emily Beale Universe

The Night Stalkers
(#1 *The Night Is Mine*)

The Night Stalkers
5D, 5E & CSAR
Stories

Night Stalkers
Holidays

Delta Force

Firehawks

Delta Force
Stories

Smokejumpers

Henderson's
Ranch

Fire Lookouts,
Hotshots,
& Firebirds
Stories

White House
Protection Force

ShadowForce
PSI

Dilya's
Dog Force*

WHPF
Stories

The Future
Night Stalkers
Stories

* *Coming soon*

For more information and alternate reading orders, please
visit: www.mlbuchman.com/reading-order

SIGN UP FOR M. L. BUCHMAN'S NEWSLETTER TODAY

and receive:
Release News
Free Short Stories
a Free Book

Get your free book today. Do it now.
free-book.mlbuchman.com